A·D·V·E·N·T·U·R·E·S
beyond the
S·O·L·A·R
SYSTEM

PLANETRON and ME

Special thanks to Suzy Gurton, Astronomy Lecturer, Griffith Observatory, Los Angeles, California, for her valuable technical assistance.

Howdy Doody reprinted with special permission of King Features Syndicate Inc. and NBC.

Technical illustration of Planetron by Eliot R. Brown

Library of Congress Cataloging-in-Publication Data

Williams, Geoffrey T.
  Adventures beyond the solar system.

  Summary: Planetron, the transformer robot turned spacecraft, speeds Will on an exciting journey into the far reaches of our galaxy where he learns a great deal about astronomy.

  [1. Astronomy—Fiction.   2. Outer space—Fiction]
I. Morgan, Pierr, ill.   II. Title.
PZ7.W65915Ad   1988   [Fic]   88-19635
ISBN 0-8431-2298-6

A·D·V·E·N·T·U·R·E·S
beyond the
S·O·L·A·R SYSTEM
PLANETRON *and* ME

By Geoffrey T. Williams

Illustrated by Pierr Morgan

PRICE STERN SLOAN
Los Angeles

H O W · B I G · I S · B I G

Someday, maybe thousands of years from now, some space traveler is going to find a brown paper bag with a sandwich and a cookie inside in orbit around a star named X-1, in the constellation Cygnus. I hope whoever it is doesn't try to pick it up. When I dropped it, I wasn't about to try—you see, Cygnus X-1 is a black hole in space . . .

The whole thing started because I had to figure out how to get to Baltimore.

"Are you done with your homework yet, Will?" Mom called from down the hallway.

"Almost, Mom." I looked back down at the paper where I'd been scribbling problems." . . . So, at eighty miles-per-hour, Mr. Smith's train gets to Baltimore forty-five minutes ahead of Mr. Johnson's. There. Done. These word problems are tricky, Planetron."

Planetron was perched on the desk, his little motors humming quietly. In case you missed my first adventure I guess I'd better explain: Planetron is my transformer robot. He looks like most other transformer robots—all red and black and silver and shiny with little wheels and antennas and lights and things.

I remember the day Dad gave him to me. "Look, Will. It says right here on the box—Exciting! Fun! Educational! Planetron, the one-of-a-kind science teacher!" And I remember thinking that Planetron looked, I don't know, mysterious and different somehow. It didn't take me long to find out just how different he was.

"Rrrr-wzz-spt." That little metallic buzzing sound is one of the ways he's different—he talks. And he's powered by sunlight, so at night I have to remember to plug him in.

"Sorry, Planetron. There you go."

"Ssszt! Thhha-spt. Thang." His batteries were charging up. "Thangg-yyooo, Wuuh. Rrremember, Www-ill, w-w-word problems provide the foundation in logical thinking and mathematical reasoning necessary for your scientific education."

I closed my math book. "Sure. But I'll probably never use any of this stuff in real life. And anyway, why would I want to go to Baltimore?"

I could hear Planetron's electronic circuits opening and closing. "But what if you wanted to go to Rigel Kent?"

"Dad uses a travel agent. I could just call her."

"I doubt if they could help you, Will. Rigel Kent is a star, usually called Alpha Centauri, in the southern Milky Way."

"I've heard of Alpha Centauri. It's the star closest to Earth."

"Actually, Will, the sun is the closest star to Earth."

"Oh. Yeah. Sure. What's the Milky Way?"

"A galaxy—a huge collection of stars, gas and dust clouds. Turn out the lights and I'll show you."

When the room was dark I heard a low humming sound and suddenly a beam of light shot out of Planetron's eyes like lightning. I jumped back. Wow! I didn't know he could do that! Right in the middle of my room, a picture formed—like a three-dimensional slide show: A beautiful band of glowing clouds about six feet across hung in the air. It was thinner at the edges and the middle was round, like a ball, and glowing brighter than the rest. There were dark patches in it, and bright colored lights— green and orange and blue. "That's the Milky Way?" I asked.

"This is a holographic picture that shows what the Milky Way looks like from far out in space as you look at the edge of it, Will."

"How big is it? How many miles across?"

"It's so big that astronomers don't measure distances in space in miles. They measure distances by how far light travels in one year."

"That's called a light year, isn't it?" I asked.

"Yes. The Milky Way is about ten thousand light years thick and 100 thousand light years across, and light travels approximately 186 thousand miles-per-second, or about six million million miles in a year—that's a six followed by twelve zeroes."

"So light from the sun has to travel through space for six million million multiplied by 100 thousand to get to the other side of the galaxy?"

"Well, since the earth is located about two-thirds of the way across the galaxy, you really only need to multiply by sixty-seven thousand."

I looked at Planetron. "Thanks. That makes it a lot easier. And those clouds of light . . . I'll bet they're not clouds . . . they're stars, right?"

"The Milky Way contains over 100 billion stars, Will."

I looked at the luminous picture hanging in the air in the middle of my room, then at the real stars outside, trying to understand numbers that big. It was hard. Let's see, I'm ten, that's a one followed by one zero . . .

Planetron turned the display until I was looking at it face-on. It looked like a giant pinwheel with glowing spokes curving out from the center like arms.

"The Milky Way is called a spiral galaxy, Will, because of the shape the arms make. The bright center is called the nucleus."

"Where's the sun?" I asked.

"It's located in one of the outer spiral arms, about thirty thousand light years from the nucleus, just about here." A tiny glowing dot appeared on the pinwheel. "The earth is ninety-

three million miles away from the sun. Its light reaches us in about eight minutes. Seven hours later the light reaches Pluto . . ."

"The planet furthest from the sun," I interrupted.

"Right. And that same light, traveling to Alpha Centauri, doesn't get there for almost four and one-third years."

Four and one-third light years! That sounded impossibly far away. With a click, the picture disappeared and the humming stopped. In the silence I heard his voice, "Fortunately, it won't take us nearly that long."

STAR · MISSION

I was in the kitchen early the next morning when Dad came in. He looked at my peanut butter and spaghetti sandwich and made a funny noise. "Promise you won't eat that in front of your mother or me, Will."

I laughed. He was just kidding . . . I think. "Don't worry, Dad. I'm taking it on a field trip with Planetron."

"You still enjoy that little toy, huh?"

"He's teaching me a lot, Dad."

"Well, he's certainly taught you a lot so far. Wish I knew how he did it. Your science teacher called and said he'd never had a student who knew so much about the solar system. Where are you going today?"

"Oh, just around the neighborhood." I didn't tell him it was the neighborhood beyond the solar system.

"Have fun. I'll be in the garage working on the car. Oh, and Will?" He looked at my lunch again, "If you can't finish that, uh, sandwich . . ."

"Yeah, Dad?"

"Please, don't bring it home."

After he left I licked the last of the spaghetti sauce off the lid of the peanut butter jar, jammed one of Mom's oatmeal raisin cookies in the bag, cleaned up my mess and called, "Okay, Planetron! Let's go!" He followed me out the door on his little wheels, then came to a stop in the backyard and announced, "Prepare for Star Mission Initiation." And that's when the fun started.

Planetron's a transformer robot, right? So, he began to transform. Parts just seemed to unfold, making him bigger. You've got to see it to believe it. I don't know how he does it. Even his voice changes.

"T minus two minutes." The wheels locked up into his body and big landing pods lowered. He kept getting larger and his voice kept on changing. "T minus thirty seconds." He was almost forty feet tall. A door opened in his side and a ramp slid down. "Please step aboard." I took a deep breath, tucked my lunch under my arm and walked up the ramp. The doors closed behind me.

Inside were rows of computer screens, knobs, dials and but-
tons. I stuck my lunch in the pocket of the spacesuit hanging on
one wall—the same spacesuit I'd worn on Mars. I wondered if I'd
have a chance to wear it again . . .

"T minus ten seconds and counting." Planetron's voice, the
voice of the ship, seemed to come from all around me.

"Nine."

There was the same big, padded acceleration chair.

"Eight."

I sat down and strapped myself in.

"Seven."

Planetron started to rumble.

"Six."

His space-drive was warming up.

"Five."

Last chance to change my mind.

"Four."

Did I really want to fly across the galaxy?

"Three."

Visit other stars?

"Two."

Maybe even other planets?

"One."

You bet I did!

"Ignition."

The space-drive roared, and I was pushed back in the chair.

MISTER · INC

We were far beyond the solar system. The sun was nothing but a dim point of light, exactly like thousands of others, lost in the distance behind us. Our destination, the southern Milky Way, blazed in the view-screen with the light of more stars than I'd ever seen before.

"There are so many, Planetron! How can you find just one?"

"The same way astronomers find objects with their telescopes—by using map coordinates."

"Longitude and latitude!" I said.

"Yes. Except coordinates in the sky are called *right ascension* and *declination.* We also have some help astronomers don't have." The computer screen in front of me flickered on and rows of numbers and symbols appeared. They made a strange shape—almost like a face. This was something new. "Will, say hello to our Multi-Relational Interstellar Navigational Computer—'Mr. Inc' for short. Mr. Inc, tell Will where we're headed."

The numbers flickered and changed colors and a voice, like something from inside a huge machine, growled, "Right ascension fourteen hours, thirty-six-point-two minutes. Declination minus sixty degrees, thirty-eight seconds."   Then the screen went dark.

"He doesn't seem very friendly, Planetron."

"Remember how you felt trying to figure out the trip to Baltimore? Well, Mr. Inc has to keep track of billions of different stars, hundreds or thousands of light years apart, and where they are in relation to the earth."

"Oh," I said. "I know how he feels."

"This is the constellation Centaurus." Several bright stars appeared on the view-screen.

"What exactly is a constellation, Planetron?"

"A group of stars that form a shape in the sky as seen from Earth. Most of them were named by ancient Greek astronomers. Here are some more."

"There's the Big Dipper and Orion," I said, as shapes of bright light blinked on in the view-screen.

"The Big Dipper is part of a constellation named Ursa Major; and there's Scorpius and Gemini and Leo," he added. "Now watch what happens as we get closer to Centaurus."

"The shape of the constellation . . . it's changing, Planetron!"

"That's because most of the stars that make up constellations aren't really together in space, Will. Some are closer to Earth, some are much further away. They just seem to be next to each other in the sky. The further away from Earth we get, the more their shapes change."

"What are those dark places? Aren't there any stars there?"

"There are huge clouds of gas and dust in space. When they're between us and the stars, they block much of the light."

"So space between stars isn't empty?"

"It's empty compared to the earth's atmosphere—there are only a few atoms of gas per cubic centimeter and a few specks of dust per cubic kilometer, compared to billions of molecules per cubic centimeter on Earth."

ALPHA·CENTAURI

Mr. Inc got us to Alpha Centauri right on schedule. We landed on an airless, blistered planet just in time to see the star rise against a range of jagged mountains.

Planetron used special filters, the way astronomers sometimes do to study our sun, so I could see more of Alpha Centauri's details. He turned on the exterior speakers and they crackled with static from electrical discharges in the star's atmosphere. "It looks like the sun, Planetron."

"There's one big difference, Will: Alpha Centauri is a binary star system—two stars that rotate around each other. A third star, Proxima Centauri, orbits both of them. Why not ask A-2-Z for more information?"

"Sure!" I grinned. I'd met A-2-Z, the atmospheric analyzer droid, on my first trip. Sensing equipment outside Planetron gave the little droid information which she reported in a synthesized computer voice. I pushed a button on my console and heard, "Primary star Alpha Centauri-A, spectral class G. Companion star, Alpha Centauri-B, spectral class K. Current separation, three billion kilometers. Rotational period, eighty years. Long time no see, Will."

I laughed. She remembered me, too! About that time a small red star, Alpha Centauri-B, rose above the horizon. "What are spectral classes, Planetron?"

"Color is one of the ways scientists classify stars, Will. White light, including sunlight, starlight, even light from lamps, is a combination of all different colors: violet, blue, green, yellow, orange, red and everything in between. That's called the color spectrum. You've seen rainbows."

"Sure. Right after a rainstorm. They're beautiful."

"Moisture in the air *refracts* sunlight—bends it. The light separates into a spectrum, forming a rainbow, because each color is bent a different amount by the drops of moisture. Starlight can be split up the same way using a tool called a spectroscope, which attaches to a telescope."

"What can scientists tell from looking at a star's spectrum?"

"They can tell how old it is, how hot it is and what kind of elements it has in it."

"Are there a lot of binary stars like Alpha Centauri?"

"Scientists estimate that half to two-thirds of all the stars in the Milky Way belong to multiple-star systems."

The FTL space-drive warning bell rang. The computer screen flickered on and Mr. Inc growled, "Course setting, right ascension eighteen hours, forty-five-point-three minutes, declination plus thirty-three degrees, eighteen seconds."

BETA·LYRA

Imagine a white-hot star fifteen times the size of the sun. Pretty big, right? Next, imagine another star more than *thirty* times bigger! And five times hotter! Now imagine those two stars so close they actually touch. That's what Beta Lyra looks like.

When we got closer I saw bright clouds of white, yellow, orange and red streaming off both giant stars. They formed a disk that looked kind of like the rings around Saturn—only thousands of times bigger and brighter. "It looks like they're losing all their star stuff, Planetron!"

"This is a *contact binary* system, Will. These stars are so close and orbit each other so rapidly that their outer atmospheres of gas are thrown off into space to form that ring, called an accretion disk."

I pushed A-2-Z's button and heard, "Primary star, Beta Lyra-A, spectral class B. Companion star, Beta Lyra-B, spectral class F. Separation, twenty-two million miles. Rotational period, twelve-point-nine-one days. What a merry-go-round!" she laughed in her little computer voice.

Planetron explained, "In addition to being a contact binary, Beta Lyra is also an *eclipsing binary*, because, as viewed from Earth, the stars pass in front of each other in their orbits."

"Kind of like a solar eclipse? Like when our moon passes in front of our sun?"

"Exactly. Measuring the variation in the amount of light during the eclipses helps astronomers determine how big the stars are and how fast they orbit each other—their rotational period."

THE · LIFE · OF · A · STAR

"What happens when all their atmosphere spins off?"

"The stars die, Will."

That sounded impossible. "But ... stars can't die, Planetron."

"Just like everything else in nature, Will, stars are born, grow old and die. I'll show you."

The view-screen lit up to show a dim disk rotating slowly in black space. "Hydrogen gas and dust floating in interstellar space is set in motion by shockwaves, perhaps caused by a nearby star. Slowly gravity draws the gas and dust closer together, forming a disk. After millions of years this disk forms a ball. As gravity draws more and more material together, the ball gets hotter. When it gets hot enough, nuclear reactions start in the core and the star starts to shine. New stars that are hotter than the sun appear blue."

A bright blue star appeared on the view-screen, next to a star that looked like the sun.

"An ordinary, middle-aged star like ours appears yellow even when it's young. For the next five billion years or so there isn't much change. But eventually, much of the hydrogen gas in the core is converted to helium and other, heavier elements such as silicon, carbon and iron. As the core gets heavier, it gets hotter, causing the star's atmosphere to expand. It becomes a *red giant* star, and can get big enough to fill up space out to the orbit of Venus. Bigger, hotter stars could be as big as our entire solar system."

An immense, dull red star appeared. "Then it begins to cool off and shrink again. A star can expand and shrink several times in its lifetime. But eventually, after much of its fuel is burned up, the star expels most of its outer atmosphere and shrinks down to become a white dwarf star about the size of the earth. Eventually, after many millions of years, it becomes a black dwarf star. Just a cold dead cinder in space."

"How long do stars live?" I asked.

"An ordinary star like the sun lives about ten billion years. But stars like Beta Lyra spin off so much matter so quickly, they only live about half as long."

Mr. Inc's voice rumbled out new coordinates and I wondered what it would be like to see a star being born.

I was just about to find out.

M 42 - THE · ORION · NEBULA

A thousand light years from Earth an incredible, flaming fan shape fills the sky: the Orion Nebula. Nebula means "cloud," and that's just what this was—a gas and dust cloud over forty light years in diameter; inside, stars were blazing to life.

Planetron explained, "Hot young stars cause the clouds of gas and dust that they were born in to glow—similar to the way electrical current causes gas to shine in a fluorescent light. How about a look inside?"

A-2-Z gave an excited yelp and I tightened my seat belt as we plunged into the heart of the enormous nebula.

We were inside the Orion Nebula, in a place called the Trapezium.

The atmosphere around us was ominous—like a sky filled with storm clouds—only these clouds were incandescent gas. Planetron said the temperature was almost eighteen thousand degrees Fahrenheit. Not nearly as hot as a star, but when I pushed A-2-Z's button she said, "Forget it, Charlie! I'm not going out there. Get Inky to do it." A deep rumble came from Mr. Inc. "Okay, okay. Mister Inc," she said.

"Come on, A-2-Z, I just want to know what that gas is. Besides, Planetron's shields protect us."

She let out an electronic sigh, "One moment, please." There were little clicks and buzzes. Then she announced, "Main components: hydrogen and helium. Traces of oxygen, nitrogen,

neon, formaldehyde, carbon monoxide, ammonia, water and methyl alcohol."

I saw several brilliant points of hot, blue light—young stars, Planetron said, that are still condensing, pulling interstellar material together, getting hotter and bigger.

The view-screen was filled with colors. Blue, white, red, orange yellow and green. Planetron said different gases glowed different colors when bombarded with ultraviolet light from the young stars. "Astronomers think some of these stars are less than 500 thousand years old, Will. One may be only two thousand years old."

The Orion Nebula was a huge nursery for new stars!

THE · HORSEHEAD · NEBULA

We were still in the constellation of Orion, about 100 light years from the Orion Nebula, when I saw something amazing. "Planetron look! It's like a painting! A gigantic painting of a horse's head!"

The vast shape filling the view-screen was silhouetted against a background of glowing gas clouds.

"The Horsehead Nebula is called a 'dark' nebula, Will. It's a dark cloud of swirling gas that scientists think could be another place where new stars will form."

"But why does it look like that?"

"Pure chance, Will. It's swirling at about fifteen-miles-per-second, so in a few thousand years it won't look like a horse anymore—it's just like a cloud on Earth that loses its shape as breezes blow it across the sky."

Mr. Inc announced, "Set course eighteen hours, fifty-one-point-seven minutes, plus thirty-two degrees, fifty-eight seconds," and we were off again.

M 57 - THE · RING · NEBULA

"What do the 'M' numbers mean, Planetron?"

"Back in 1781 a French astronomer and comet-hunter named Charles Messier catalogued 107 objects in the sky that he thought might be confused with comets. Astronomers have new cataloging systems for stars now, but we still use the 'M' from Messier's name plus his numbering system for many of the objects."

"Doesn't that get confusing?" I asked.

Planetron chuckled, "Over the centuries astronomers have done things much more confusing than that, Will. I'll give you an example when we land."

The motors died down and I felt a gentle thump. He set us down on a large asteroid. When the view-screen brightened I saw a dead, brown landscape, pitted with old impact craters like the earth's moon. Then the cameras shifted and I saw the most amazing thing . . . a fantastic ring hanging out in space, with one bright star right in the center!

"This is M 57, the Ring Nebula in the constellation Lyra. It's called a *planetary nebula* because years ago astronomers mistook the rounded shape in their small telescopes for a distant planet."

"It's beautiful, but how did it get like that?"

"One theory is that when the larger star in a binary system collapses from a red giant to a white dwarf, the companion star orbits inside the atmosphere the collapsing giant leaves behind, causing it to disintegrate. As this happens the companion star violently spins off its own gases and the atmospheres of both stars boil out into space, creating this huge bubble. Ultraviolet radiation from the white dwarf causes the different gases—hydrogen, helium, oxygen, nitrogen, sulphur and neon—to glow in different colors."

"It doesn't look like a bubble, Planetron. It looks like a ring."

"That's because you see a larger area of gases around the edges than through the front and back. Like you see the outlines of a soap bubble."

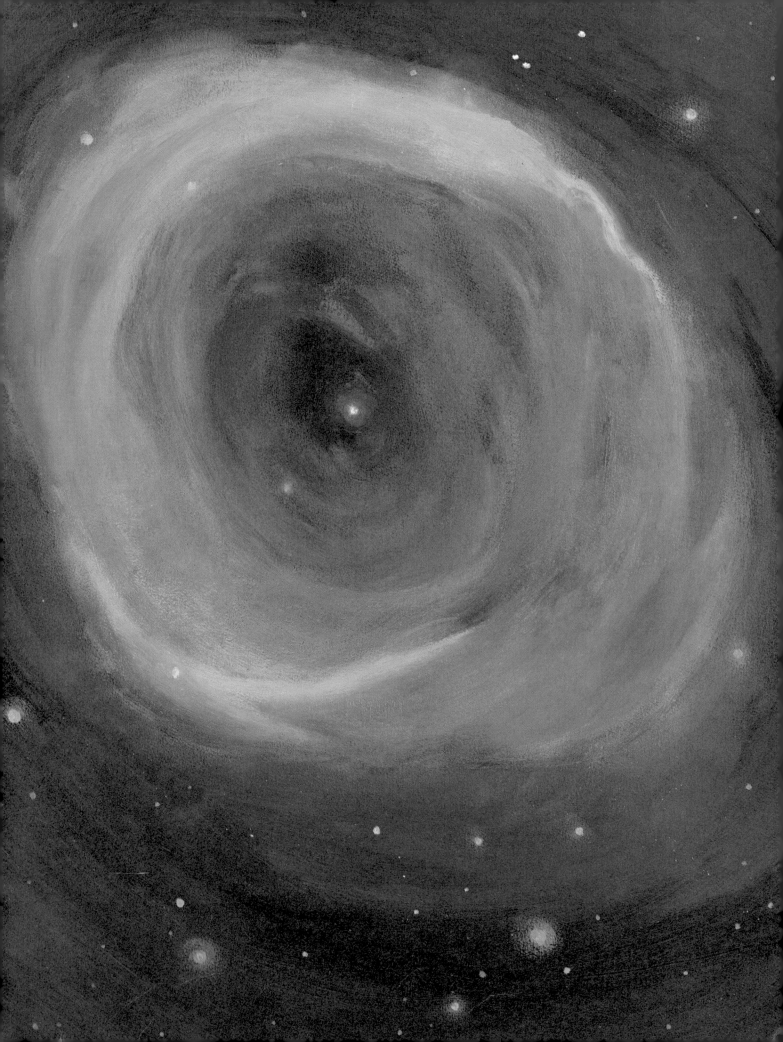

THE · WHITE · DWARF

Planetron flew us through the bubble of expanding gas surrounding the small hot star. From the inside it was like being behind a gigantic, glowing curtain. The star at the center was only about as big as the earth, but it glowed much brighter than our sun.

"Interior temperature 100 thousand degrees. Now we're cookin'!" A-2-Z reported.

Planetron said, "Matter in white dwarf stars is so condensed that just a teaspoon of it weighs thousands of pounds."

"Were there ever any planets around it, like in our solar system?"

"If there were, they would have been burned to cinders when the star became a red giant."

"Is our sun going to become a white dwarf, Planetron?"

"Many scientists think so, Will. But we don't have to worry for a few billion years or so."

"Are there other planets like Earth in the galaxy?"

"There are many planets in the Milky Way, Will. There must be some that are similar to Earth."

"Could we find one?" I asked.

He was quiet for a moment. Then, instead of a simple yes or no, he said, "Will, why don't you consider what you know about the earth, the solar system, the galaxy and stars and then tell me and Mr. Inc where to look."

THE · SEARCH · BEGINS

It was up to me to find a new planet! It was kind of like solving word problems. "Well, since it has to be a planet humans can live on, its sun should be pretty much like ours. It can't be too old, like the white dwarf star in the middle of the Ring Nebula. And it can't be too young like the new stars in the Trapezium. Humans couldn't live near them . . ."

"We need a *main sequence* star," said Planetron. "One that's about middle-aged. I'll feed the data to Mr. Inc." The interstellar navigational computer flickered to life and gave a low growl—like he was hungry for information.

I thought some more, "It can't be too hot or cold . . ."

"Somewhere between spectral classes F and K," said Planetron. That got fed into Mr. Inc, too. "Now, how about the planet's orbit around the sun, Will?"

"Well, if it's too close, it'll be too hot, and if it's too far away, it'll be too cold."

"About one AU—that's astronomical unit—from its sun. Ninety-three million miles, give or take a bit . . . " Planetron said, feeding more data to Mr. Inc. "That eliminates about ninety percent of all the stars in the Milky Way."

"Great!" I said, thinking the search wouldn't take long.

Mr. Inc hiccupped and made a sound like . . . well, like an electronic burp.

Planetron said, "Good. Mr. Inc says we only have to search through about ten billion solar systems."

"Gee. That *is* good, Planetron. Only ten bill . . . ten billion?! But . . . but . . . we'll never find a planet!"

A-2-Z spoke up, "If anyone can find us one, Inky can!"

"While we're waiting we can see a few more things," said Planetron.

M 13 · IN · HERCULES

We flew trillions of miles above the plane of the Milky Way. Centered in the view-screen was a hazy ball of light. As we got closer, I saw it was really thousands and thousands of stars.

"Is that another galaxy, Planetron?"

"No. That is M 13, a globular cluster. One of about one hundred that orbit around the Milky Way."

The sky blazed with the light of the stars we flashed past. I saw planetary nebulas, white dwarfs, red giants and plenty of yellow and orange stars like our sun.

"Astronomers think globular clusters contain the oldest stars in the galaxy, Will. Almost as old as the Milky Way itself."

"How old is that?"

"Over fifteen billion years." Thump. We landed on an asteroid orbiting a star close to the center of M 13.

I could hardly believe my ears when Planetron said, "I think your spacesuit still fits you, Will."

I was nervous. I hadn't worn my spacesuit since I'd been on Mars. I'd had plenty of problems that first time, but at least on Mars there was enough gravity to remind me which way was up—here there was none. Zero gravity. I didn't weigh anything at all! I found that out when I stood up too fast and sailed out of the chair. "Whoa!" My arms and legs whirled like a windmill. To stop myself, I pushed my hands against the ceiling. Boy, was that a mistake! I went flapping back the other way—upside down! A-2-Z was laughing and, along with feeling silly, I was getting dizzy. I finally realized I could control myself by gentle pushes in the direction I wanted to go. After that it didn't take too long to get over to the spacesuit hanging in its special storage closet. I stepped in and pulled the suit up around me.

Each boot had small patches of Velcro on the bottom which stuck to Velcro strips on the floor, the walls, even the ceiling! At least I wouldn't fall down anymore.

I sealed the face plate. The spacesuit automatically began feeding air to the helmet. It hissed quietly. There was a drinking tube close to my mouth, and a radio transmitter switch I could turn on just by pressing my chin against it.

"Communication systems check," Planetron's voice said thinly in my ears.

I chinned the transmitter switch. "Will to Planetron. Do you read me?" I'd heard them talk like that on TV.

"Loud and clear, Will. Step into the airlock, please."

A door slid open and I went into the small airlock chamber. The door shut with a solid click. There was a "whoosh" as Planetron opened air valves and equalized the pressure in the chamber.

On Mars I had gone out in a little robot explorer vehicle called X-Bot. Not this time. There was a long cable attached to the side of the ship and Planetron had me hook it to my suit. Without it I might just float away in space forever.

"Will? What's that in the pocket of your spacesuit?" Planetron asked.

I'd forgotten all about my lunch. "Just a sandwich."

"Oh. What kind?"

"Peanut butter and spaghetti."

Planetron made the same kind of sound my father had made. "Perhaps you should leave it here in the airlock."

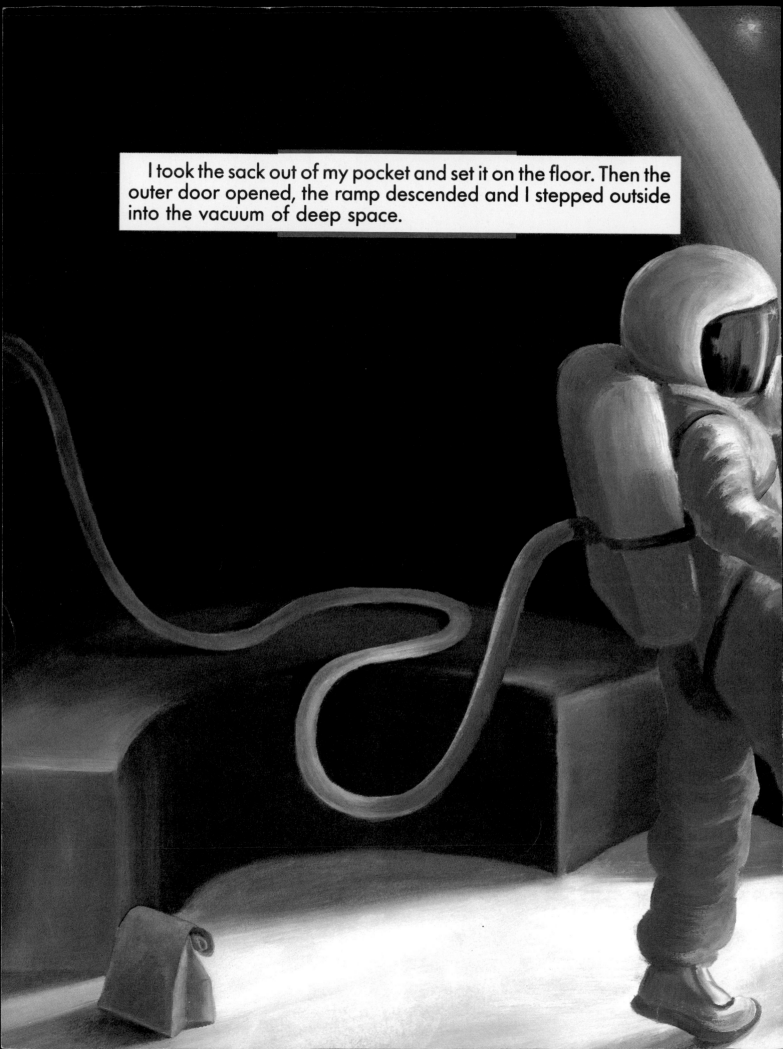

I took the sack out of my pocket and set it on the floor. Then the outer door opened, the ramp descended and I stepped outside into the vacuum of deep space.

I pushed off from the ramp and floated up slowly, the cable trailing out behind me like a long tail. Soon I was far above Planetron with nothing between me and tens of thousands of stars.

From horizon to horizon, as far as I could see, the sky was filled with brilliant points of light—stars as thick as grains of sand on the beach. Nowhere in the galaxy, except maybe in the very center, are the stars so tightly packed. It was amazing. "Planetron, is it day or night here?"

"It will always be night here, Will. This solar system's star is almost dead."

I looked around. Finally, I found it. This star was almost a black dwarf—smaller than our sun and nearly invisible. Its surface was

glowing a dim, dull red, like a lump of coal cooling in a fireplace.

"It used up the very last of its nuclear fuel long ago, Will. Now it only shines because of the thermal energy created by its condensed gases."

I pulled myself back down the cable. The airlock doors closed and Planetron equalized the pressure. Before long, I was sitting in the acceleration chair. "Do all stars just fade away like that when they die, Planetron?"

"No, Will. Some have incredibly violent deaths. They're called supernovas. When you're strapped in I'll show you the most famous one." As we lifted off and the countless stars of M 13 flashed past, I could hear Mr. Inc grumble and growl, continuing the planet search.

M1 - THE · CRAB

I almost jumped out of my seat when the alarm went off. I heard A-2-Z warn, "Forbidden Zone. Entry prohibited. Forbidden Zone. Entry prohibited . . ."

"What's wrong, Planetron?"

"We're getting close to the Crab Nebula—a very strong source of x-rays. My shields protect us, but I don't want to get too close."

"What's the Crab Nebula?"

The view-screen brightened and I saw a tattered and jagged cloud glowing with bright threads of colored gases. It looked weird and twisted and violent.

"It's the remains of an exploded star called a supernova—one of the most violent events in all of nature. When a star two or three times more massive than our sun explodes and collapses it releases more energy than a billion ordinary stars put together."

"Would I be able to see it from Earth?"

"Yes. Just like Yang Wei-Te did. He was the keeper of the Chinese calendar who first reported what he thought was a new star to the Chinese emperor in the year 1054. In fact, the word *nova* means "new." In a few days this "new" star became brighter than any star in the sky. Brighter than Venus. So bright, in fact, that it could be seen in daylight. As well as being a source of x-rays, it also sends out gamma rays and radio waves. We can hear the radio waves with special monitoring equipment. Listen."

A loud static noise came from the speakers. And something else. A fast pulsing sound. "What's that sound, Planetron?"

"It's coming from a *neutron* star at the center of the nebula—a star smaller than the state of Rhode Island, and many times denser than a white dwarf star. A teaspoon of neutron star matter would weigh more than a mountain. When it collapsed it began spinning thirty times a second. As it spins, its powerful magnetic field gives off beams of energy in the radio frequencies. Astronomers call it a pulsar—a pulsating radio source."

I could almost feel the awesome power and energy at work in the Crab Nebula. It was a little frightening, and I was glad Planetron didn't want to get too close. It was one of the strangest things I'd ever seen. But not the strangest. That was coming up.

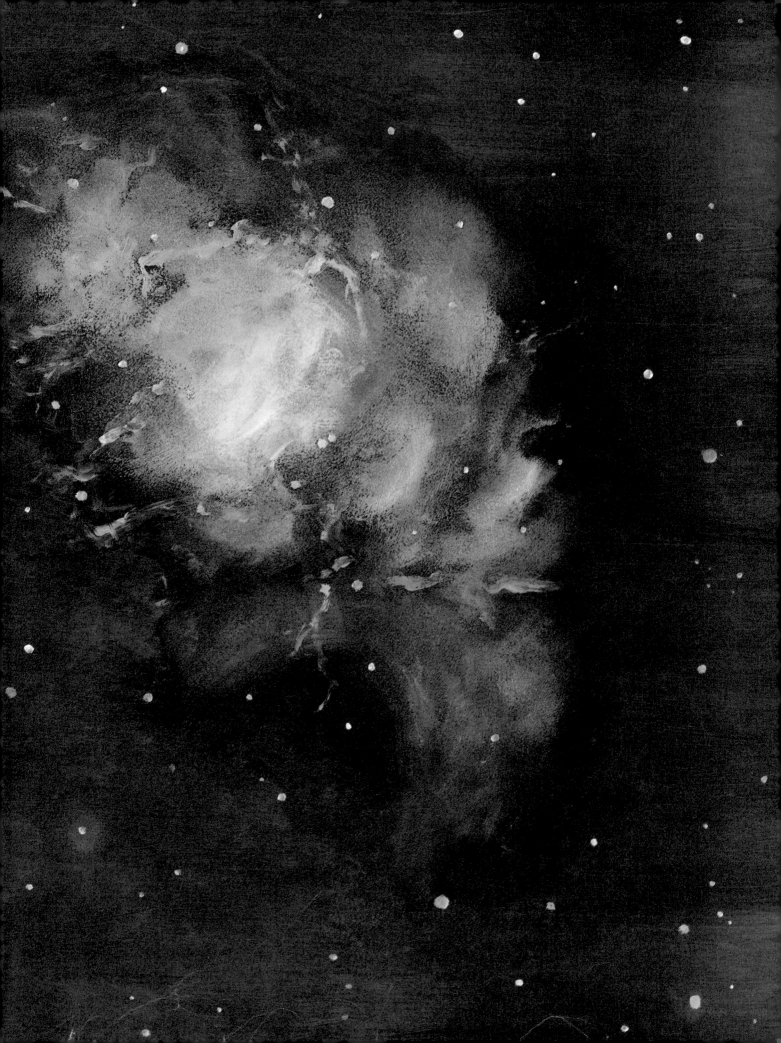

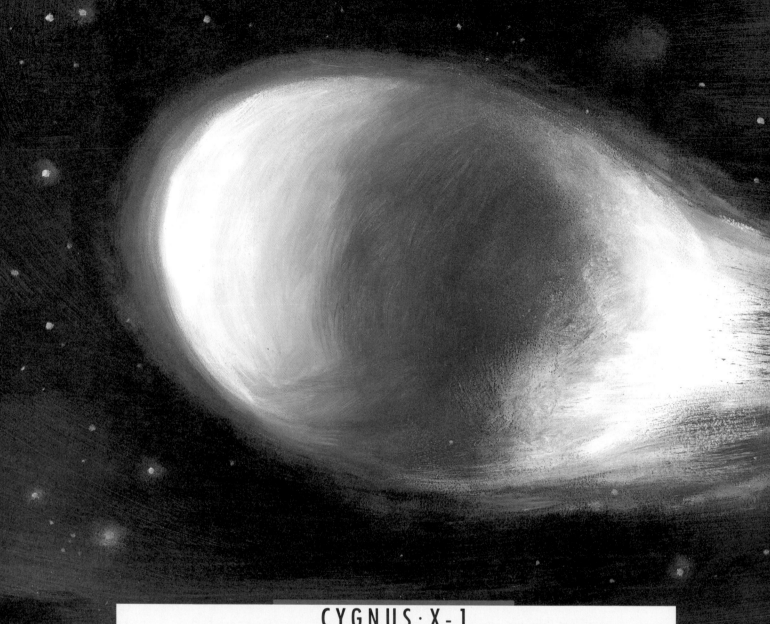

CYGNUS·X-1

Imagine a place where gravity is a hundred thousand times more powerful than on Earth. So powerful that it bends space and warps time. So powerful that anything that gets too close to it is sucked inside and disappears from our universe forever. Anything. Even light.

A place like that is called a *black hole.* And I got close to one. Almost too close.

It looked ordinary enough in the view-screen: just a hot, blue super-giant star in the constellation of Cygnus. But as we flew closer I could tell something was wrong. The star was distorted, egg-shaped. Its atmosphere was pouring off in radiant ribbons of colors, forming a huge ring, like the Beta Lyra binary system. Only this time, there wasn't another star. The gases were spinning off

and forming an accretion disk around nothing! It was revolving like a giant whirlpool in space. It was scary.

"Where's all the atmosphere going, Planetron?! What's happening?"

"At the center of that disk is a star about 300 kilometers in diameter but many times more massive than our entire solar system. It's spinning over one thousand times a second."

"Where? I can't see it."

"That's because when it collapsed, its mass created a gravity field so powerful that all light was trapped on the surface. It couldn't escape. The star just winked ouuuut oooffff ex-isssssstannnccccce."

Oh, no! What was that? Was something wrong with Planetron's voice?

"Plllaaanaaatronnn . . ." I said, then stopped. My voice sounded weird too—kind of echoing and stretched out.

The alarm went off and A-2-Z announced, "Forbiddennnn Zooonnnnne. Ennntrrry prrroohhhibiiiited . . ."

"What'ssss wrrronnng?" I yelled.

"We'rrre toooo clossse tooo the blaaack hollle, Wiiiiill. Straaap yourrrsellllf innnn. We'rrrre abooout tooo fiiinnnd ooout howww poooowerrrfulll myyyy spaaaccce-driiive iiisss."

I felt the space-drive start up, but we didn't move at all! In fact, we were being pulled closer to the black hole!

The roar of the engines deepened. The ship shuddered under the incredible power. I heard a loud noise over by the airlock, but I didn't have time to worry about it as we lurched from side to side. It felt like we were being torn apart by the gravitational currents of the invisible black hole!

Then, cutting through the noise, I heard Planetron's voice, sounding as strong and confident as ever, "Heeerrreee weeee goooooo."

There was a thunderous explosion of sound. Planetron shook violently. Then, in the view-screen, I could see us pulling slowly away from the black hole.

Whew! That was a close call!

When we were safe again I let out my breath in a sigh of relief. "What happened back there, Planetron?"

"I'm not sure, Will. So little is known about black holes. It seemed as though our sense of time was distorted—drawn out somehow. My sensors didn't react quickly enough to warn us we were getting too close. I'm monitoring damage control now." I heard some quiet electronic squeaks and squawks. Then he said "We sustained some very minor damage. It seems the outer airlock door was shaken open, and . . ."

A-2-Z interrupted him, "You just lost your lunch, Will!"

I laughed until I had to wipe tears from my eyes.

A short time later Mr. Inc rumbled and announced, "Planet confirmation. Course settings being determined."

A-2-Z let out a cheer, "I told you Inky could do it!"

Our search for an Earth-like planet was over.

TERRA·NOVA

The planet beneath us was so beautiful it made me homesick.
We were in a solar system about seventy thousand light years across the Milky Way from Earth. In many ways, this system was like ours. In other ways, it was strangely different.

The sun was an F5 spectral type—slightly hotter than ours, and a few million years younger. There were several gas-giant planets in distant orbits, including one almost twice as big as Jupiter. The Earth-like planets orbited closer to the sun. There was one four times the size of Earth, but so far away from the sun that its immense surface would remain frozen forever.

We called the planet Mr. Inc had found "Terra Nova," which means "new earth." It was a little larger than Earth and closer to its sun—about eighty-five million miles away. Two moons, both larger than ours, circled the planet. On our approach I watched the blurred shapes of continents beneath white clouds; wide rivers ran through heavy forests and rolling green hills to distant, deep blue oceans.

A-2-Z spoke up, "Main atmospheric components-nitrogen and oxygen. Surface temperature 75 degrees. Surf's up, Will."

I smiled. She was right. A line of white-tipped waves crashed against a sandy shoreline far below; clouds pushed against a sharp ridge of mountains which ran like a backbone across this huge continent. "Planetron, are there people down there?"

"I don't know, Will."

"Can we land and find out?"

He paused before answering. "I know you'd like to, Will. In some ways, so would I. But I don't think it would be wise. This is a younger solar system than ours. If there is a civilization there ... well ... you wouldn't want to startle anyone, would you?"

"No ... I guess not. But wouldn't it be great to find an advanced civilization? One we could talk with?"

"That would be one of the most important events in our history, Will."

As we orbited I asked, "How would you recognize an advanced civilization?"

"On Earth we use energy in the electromagnetic spectrum to transmit our communications. If other intelligent life forms do too, we might recognize them by their broadcasts."

"You mean radio and TV shows?" I asked, amazed.

"That's right."

I had to think about that one. What kind of shows would they have? Game shows? Beauty pageants? MTV?

Mr. Inc gave the new coordinates for Earth and soon Terra Nova was far behind us. I wish Planetron would have let us land. Well, maybe next time.

SIGNS·OF·INTELLEGENCE

All at once the computer screens, instrument lights, even the big view-screen, started to pulse—bright, dim, bright, dim. And a low, warbling tone came over the speakers.

"What is it, Planetron? Are we in trouble?"

"One moment, Will. Click. Whizz. Buzz. Sensors have detected an electronic transmission indicating intelligent life forms."

"Intelligent life forms? You mean aliens? Where from? What do they look like?"

The pulsing lights stopped. There was a buzzing noise, like static from a distant radio station, and wavy lines appeared on the view-screen. A picture was forming! I couldn't wait! A giant face came into focus. "Gee, Planetron, it looks weird. Almost human . . . but not quite . . . are those freckles? There's something familiar about that face . . ." Suddenly the sound boomed into the control room loud and clear. It was a song!

"It's Howdy-Doody time! It's Howdy-Doody time! It's Howdy-Doody time! It's Howdy-Doody time!"

I was beginning to understand. "Planetron, that's not an alien language. That's English, isn't it? But what's a Howdy Doody?"

Planetron chuckled. "Will, unless I'm mistaken, it's an early children's TV cartoon show from Earth. Let me check our location with Mr. Inc."

The navigator grumbled and rumbled, and then announced, "Distance from Earth, approximately forty light years."

"That's about right, Will. Earth has been sending radio waves into space since the 1920s and TV broadcasts since the 1940s."

A strange thought came to me. "That means if there's another civilization on a planet within forty light years of Earth, they could be receiving this TV show?"

"Along with many other broadcasts, Will. The music of Beethoven and Mozart, presidential inaugurations, TV news programs . . ."

"News about wars and fighting, too?"

"I'm afraid so."

"I wonder what they think of us, Planetron?"

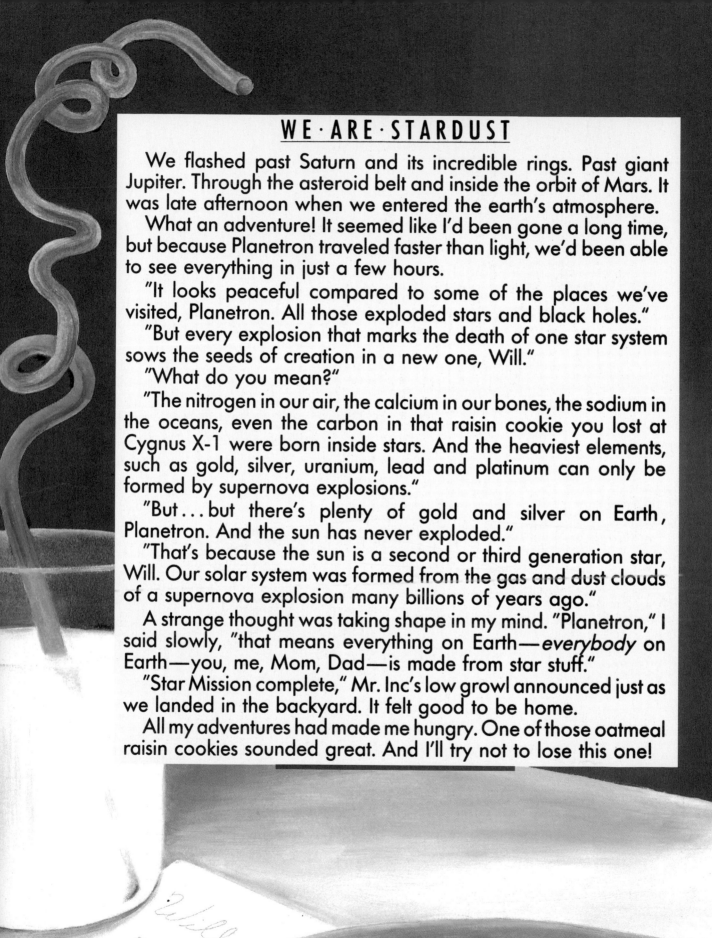

WE · ARE · STARDUST

We flashed past Saturn and its incredible rings. Past giant Jupiter. Through the asteroid belt and inside the orbit of Mars. It was late afternoon when we entered the earth's atmosphere.

What an adventure! It seemed like I'd been gone a long time, but because Planetron traveled faster than light, we'd been able to see everything in just a few hours.

"It looks peaceful compared to some of the places we've visited, Planetron. All those exploded stars and black holes."

"But every explosion that marks the death of one star system sows the seeds of creation in a new one, Will."

"What do you mean?"

"The nitrogen in our air, the calcium in our bones, the sodium in the oceans, even the carbon in that raisin cookie you lost at Cygnus X-1 were born inside stars. And the heaviest elements, such as gold, silver, uranium, lead and platinum can only be formed by supernova explosions."

"But . . . but there's plenty of gold and silver on Earth, Planetron. And the sun has never exploded."

"That's because the sun is a second or third generation star, Will. Our solar system was formed from the gas and dust clouds of a supernova explosion many billions of years ago."

A strange thought was taking shape in my mind. "Planetron," I said slowly, "that means everything on Earth—*everybody* on Earth—you, me, Mom, Dad—is made from star stuff."

"Star Mission complete," Mr. Inc's low growl announced just as we landed in the backyard. It felt good to be home.

All my adventures had made me hungry. One of those oatmeal raisin cookies sounded great. And I'll try not to lose this one!

PLANETRON'S GUIDE TO THE GALAXY

Key: R.A.-right ascension Dec.-declination L-Y-light years

Destination	R.A. hrs.	R.A. min.	Dec. °	Dec. ′	Distance L-Y	Other Information
Alpha Centauri	14	36.2	−60	38	4.3	Located in the constellation Centaurus. It is the third brightest star in the sky and one of the first used by astronomers to determine distances to the stars. It is a white spectral class G star, very much like the sun, temperature approximately 5000-6000° K (Kelvin).
Beta Lyra	18	48.3	+33	18	46.6	In the constellation Lyra. An eclipsing binary pair with a period of 12.9 days. The primary is a hot blue-green B class star, over 11,000° K. An important object for studying the evolution of stars.
Orion Nebula	5	32.9	−5	25	1000	The famous nebula in the constellation Orion. An emmission nebula located in the middle of Orion's sword. Easily seen with binoculars.
Horsehead Nebula	5	38.5	−2	26	1000	Also located in Orion, just below the hunter's belt.
Ring Nebula	18	51.7	+32	58	2200	Planetary Nebula located in the constellation Lyra. Scientists have located about 1000 planetary nebula in the galaxy. Important objects for studying the evolution of stars.
M 13 in Hercules	16	39.9	+36	33	22,000	Famous globular cluster in the constellation Hercules. It is over 200 light years in diameter and contains more than 1 million stars. There are more than 100 globular clusters surrounding the Milky Way. Appears as a fuzzy object in binoculars.
The Crab Nebula	5	31.5	+21	59	3900	Located in the constellation Taurus. The gases left over from this violent supernova explosion are expanding outward at over 600 miles-per-second. Supernovas that can be seen with the naked eye are very rare. But in February, 1987, one was discovered in the Large Magellanic Cloud, our nearest neighboring galaxy, just over 170,000 light years away. Scientists think it could become a pulsar like the Crab Nebula.

Cygnus X-1	20	22.6	+40	23	?	The first stellar object astronomers discovered that could be a black hole. Since gravity is so strong light cannot escape it, a black hole cannot be seen. It can only be detected by observing how it affects other objects.
Earth						A small planet orbiting an ordinary G2 spectral class star, located in an outer arm of a rather ordinary spiral galaxy known as the Milky Way. It is thought to be the home planet of the human race.

THE TWENTY BRIGHTEST STARS

Name	R.A. hrs.	min.	Dec. °	′	Mag*	Distance	Constellation
Sirius	6	42.9	−16	39	−1.42	8.7	Canis Major (Big Dog)
Canopus	6	22.8	−52	40	−0.72	230	Carina (Keel)
Alpha Centauri	14	36.2	−60	38	−0.27	4.3	Centaurus (Centaur)
Arcturus	14	13.4	+19	27	−0.06	38	Boötes (Bear Driver)
Vega	18	35.2	+38	44	0.04	27	Lyra (Lyre)
Capella	5	13.0	+45	57	0.05	46	Auriga (Charioteer)
Rigel	5	13.0	−8	15	0.14	500	Orion (Orion)
Procyon	7	36.7	+5	21	0.38	11	Canis Minor (Little Dog)
Betelgeuse	5	52.5	+7	24	0.41v	300	Orion (Orion)
Achernar	1	35.9	−57	29	0.51	73	Eridanus (River)
Beta Centauri	14	0.3	−60	8	0.63	190	Centaurus (Centaur)
Altair	19	48.3	+8	44	0.77	16	Aquila (Eagle)
Alpha Crucis	12	23.8	−62	49	0.9	220	Crux (Cross)
Aldebaran	4	33.0	+16	25	0.86	64	Taurus (Bull)
Spica	13	22.6	−10	54	0.91v	190	Virgo (Virgin)
Antares	16	26.3	−26	19	0.92	230	Scorpius (Scorpion)
Pollux	7	42.3	+28	9	1.16	33	Gemini (Twins)
Fomalhaut	22	54.9	−29	53	1.19	23	Picis Austrinus (Southern Fish)
Deneb	20	39.7	+45	6	1.26	650	Cygnus (Swan)
Beta Crucis	12	44.8*	−59	25	1.28v	500	Crux (Cross)

* Magnitude is a way of telling how stars compare in brightness. The higher the number, the dimmer a star appears. A difference of 1 magnitude (such as between Alpha Centauri and Deneb) is a difference in brightness of 2.512 times. The unaided human eye can see stars as dim as 6 magnitudes, which is 100 times dimmer than a first magnitude star. A large telescope can take pictures of stars millions of times too dim for the human eye to see. A "v" next to a magnitude indicates a variable star.

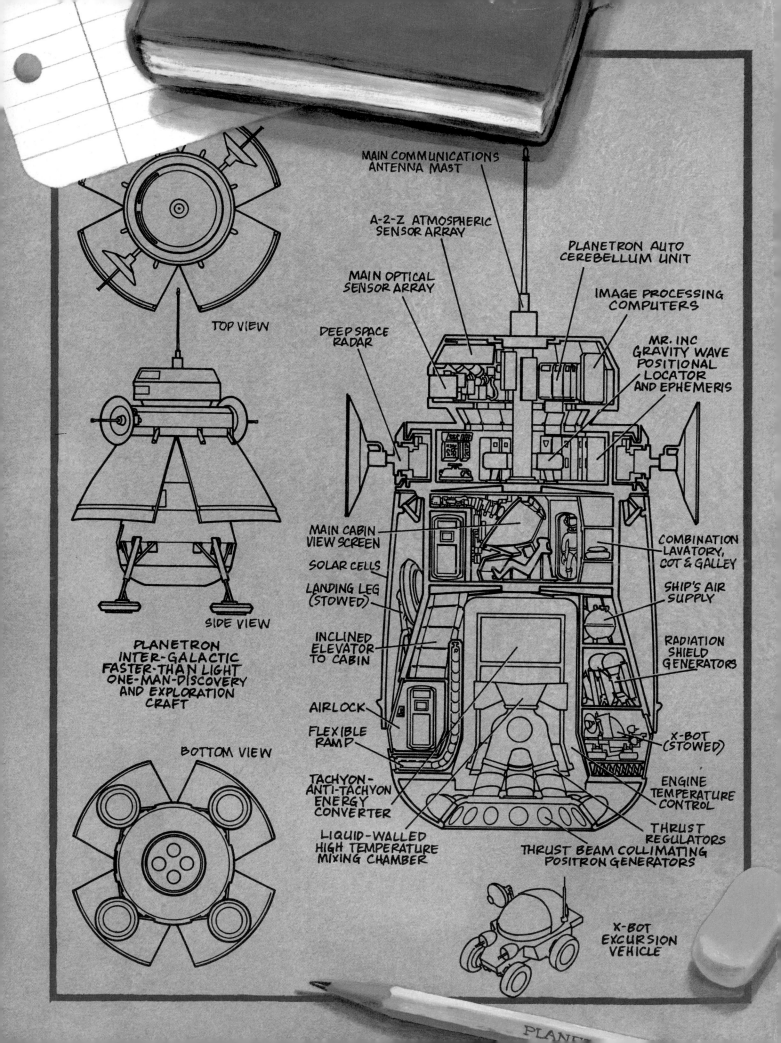

TOP VIEW

SIDE VIEW

PLANETRON
INTER-GALACTIC
FASTER-THAN LIGHT
ONE-MAN-DISCOVERY
AND EXPLORATION
CRAFT

BOTTOM VIEW

MAIN COMMUNICATIONS
ANTENNA MAST

A-2-Z ATMOSPHERIC
SENSOR ARRAY

PLANETRON AUTO
CEREBELLUM UNIT

MAIN OPTICAL
SENSOR ARRAY

IMAGE PROCESSING
COMPUTERS

DEEP SPACE
RADAR

MR. INC
GRAVITY WAVE
POSITIONAL
LOCATOR
AND EPHEMERIS

MAIN CABIN
VIEW SCREEN

COMBINATION
LAVATORY,
COT & GALLEY

SOLAR CELLS

SHIP'S AIR
SUPPLY

LANDING LEG
(STOWED)

RADIATION
SHIELD
GENERATORS

INCLINED
ELEVATOR
TO CABIN

AIRLOCK

X-BOT
(STOWED)

FLEXIBLE
RAMP

ENGINE
TEMPERATURE
CONTROL

TACHYON-
ANTI-TACHYON
ENERGY
CONVERTER

THRUST
REGULATORS

LIQUID-WALLED
HIGH TEMPERATURE
MIXING CHAMBER

THRUST BEAM COLLIMATING
POSITRON GENERATORS

X-BOT
EXCURSION
VEHICLE

PLANE